See what great love the Father has lavished on us, that we should be called children of God! *And that is what we are!*

—1 JOHN 3:1

WHO GOD WANTS ME TO BE

WATERBROOK

written by CRYSTAL BOWMAN and MICHELLE S. LAZUREK

SANDRA EIDE

MUSICIAN
CONSTRUCTION
Fire
Fighter
Vet
Magician
BALLET
Actress
Athlete
Coach

I'm **Haley**. I love to help people when they're not feeling well.

My grandpa has a bad cough. I use my stethoscope
to listen to his chest.

"One day, I'm going to be a doctor," I tell him.
"Then I can give medicine to people who are sick."

"God gave you a tender heart, Haley," Grandpa says.
"You would be a great doctor."

I spin around and close my eyes. I imagine wearing a
white coat with a real stethoscope around my neck.

"Time to visit the next patient!"

But maybe I'll become **an architect** and design a hospital for sick children.

A hospital needs lots of rooms so kids can play with toys
and have their families close by.

And every room needs a big window so the **sun can shine in**.

Or maybe I'll be **a dentist** so I can help people have happy smiles.
I'll give each of my patients a new toothbrush and tell them,

"Brush your teeth twice a day to keep those cavities away!"

Whatever job I do when I grow up, **I want to care for people**, just like God does.

I'll keep trusting God, and then I will see exactly who he wants **me to be**.

I'm **Isabela**. I like to play school.

hello
hola

I write spelling words on the
chalkboard to help my students learn.

I spin my globe and look at all the different countries where they speak Spanish, like I do at home. "Hola, ¿cómo están?" I say.

Every weekend I teach Sunday school too.
"¡Cristo les ama!"

But maybe I'll be **a mom who stays home with her children**.

We'll read bedtime stories and imagine exciting adventures.
We'll go for walks and find treasures to put in our pockets.

And when it's time for lunch, I'll teach my kids how to make delicious recipes my abuela taught me.

Or maybe **I'll open a soup kitchen** so I can feed families who are hungry.

Every Friday at the local shelter, my papi and I serve bowls of soup and rice to people who need a hot meal, and we pray with them before they eat.

We smile as friends hug each other and kids run up and down between the tables.

Whatever job I have, **I want to give people hope** for the future, just like God does.

I'll keep trusting God, and then I will see exactly who he wants **me to be.**

I'm **Lexi**. I like to create pictures on my easel.

My grandma gives me lots of paint and paper.

As I stir the colors, I imagine my art in a gallery.

I paint pink-and-orange sunsets, snowcapped mountains, and ocean waves splashing on rocks.

I want my creations to remind people of God's **beautiful designs**.

But maybe I'll make beautiful music for God.
I hop onto the piano bench in my living room and
play the keys quickly, humming along.

When I sing songs for God, I feel close to him.
I imagine I'm at church, clapping and dancing
to the music with my friends.

Or maybe **I'll own a construction company** and build homes for families.
"Looks like that house needs some paint," I'll tell the builders.

My painting crew will be ready with ladders
and brushes and gallons of paint.

When the house is ready, the family will move in.

Whatever I do, **I want to make people happy**, just like God does.

I'll keep trusting God, and then I will see exactly who he wants **me to be**.

I'm **Ashley**. I like helping God's creatures.

At the beach, I rush over to rescue a sea turtle
who's caught in some trash near the shore.
"May I keep him?" I ask.

But Mom says no. "The turtle needs to stay where God placed him.
Otherwise, he could get sick."

As I release him into the ocean, I imagine being **a vet**.

I'll give medicine to a dog who ate too many bones, and I'll wrap a bandage around a cat's injured leg.

But maybe I'll become **a firefighter** so I can protect animals and their homes from fires.

As sirens blare and flashing lights spin, I'll drive
the fire truck to the blazing forest.

I'll help my rescue team pull the giant hose to the
trees and spray water to put out the flames.

Or maybe **I'll train service dogs** for people who need their help.

"This guide dog will help you get where you want to go," I'll tell a boy who is blind. "This alert dog will let you know when someone rings your doorbell," I'll say to a grandma who has trouble hearing.

My service dogs will make life easier for many people and will become their friends too.

Whatever I become someday, **I want to care for all creatures**, just like God does.

I'll keep trusting God, and then I will see exactly who he wants **me to be**.

I want to **help** people and animals **too**. I want to tell children,

"Jesus loves you."

I want to do the **best** that I can.

I know that GOD LOVES ME and has **a good PLAN.**

I'll keep trusting God,

and then I will see exactly who he wants **ME TO BE.**

HEY, GIRLS!

Do you wonder what you'll be when you grow up?
You don't have to decide now, and you might change
your mind many times.

CRYSTAL BOWMAN

I loved playing with my dolls and stuffed animals when I was a young girl. I pretended I was a teacher and they were my students. I would tell them stories that I had made up and teach them happy songs. When I grew up, I taught preschool, Sunday school, and Bible school. Now I visit children at schools and teach them how to write poetry. I also teach adults how to write for children, and I write books to help children learn more about God. Keep exploring and dreaming and learning new things. Talk to God often and tell him what's on your heart and mind. Ask God for wisdom to make good choices and trust him to guide you one step at a time.

MICHELLE S. LAZUREK

When I was a little girl, I dreamed of being an actress and a singer. I spent hours in my room belting out my favorite tunes into my hairbrush, imagining I was singing songs on a big stage, or I was creating plays and skits and performing them with my stuffed animals. Today, I serve on my church's worship team, singing songs that honor God rather than myself. And I also create books that promote a positive Christian message. No dream is too big, so let your imagination go wild! Whatever you do, be open to what God has for your life, because he always has a plan just as he promises in his Word.

As you grow and learn, you'll discover the talents and desires God has given you. You'll find out what you enjoy doing and how you can share God's love with others. God is pleased when we use his gifts to do good things!

But more than anything else, God wants you to be **his child**—and you can do that

RIGHT NOW!

Crystal

Michelle